TOLONO PUBLIC LIBRARY

W9-CUR-304

FEB   2009
JAN 0 5 2011   AUG 15 21 2016
                    OCT 19 2016
MAR 1 7 2011
    APR 0 9 2011   SEP 2 8 2017
                    DEC 0 2017
    FEB 1 1 2012   MAY 1 0 2019
MAY 2 9 2012   JUL 15 2019
FEB 0 6 2013
GAYLORD OCT 0 1 2013   PRINTED IN U.S.A.

TOLONO PUBLIC LIBRARY

Cornelius

DRAGONFLY BOOKS™ PUBLISHED BY ALFRED A. KNOPF, INC.

Copyright © 1983 by Leo Lionni

All rights reserved under International and Pan-American Copyright
Conventions. Published in the United States of America by Alfred A.
Knopf, Inc., New York, and simultaneously in Canada by Random House of
Canada Limited, Toronto. Distributed by Random House, Inc., New York.
Originally published in hardcover by Pantheon Books in 1983.

Library of Congress Catalog Card Number: 82-6442
ISBN: 0-679-86040-1
First Dragonfly Books edition: April 1994

Manufactured in the U.S.A.
20 19 18 17 16 15 14 13 12

Cornelius

a fable by Leo Lionni

Dragonfly Books™ • Alfred A. Knopf • New York

When the eggs hatched,
the little crocodiles crawled out
onto the riverbeach.
But Cornelius walked out *upright*.

As he grew taller and stronger
he rarely came down on all fours.
He saw things no other
crocodile had ever seen before.
"I can see far beyond the bushes!"
he said.
But the others said,
"What's so good about that?"

"I can see the fish from above!" Cornelius said.
"So what?" said the others, annoyed.

And so one day, Cornelius angrily decided to walk away.

It was not long before he met a monkey.
"I can walk upright!" Cornelius said proudly.
"And I can see things far away!"

TORONTO PUBLIC LIBRARY

"I can stand on my head," said the monkey.

"And hang from my tail."
Cornelius was amazed. "Could I learn to do that?" he asked.

"Of course," replied the monkey.
"All you need is a lot of hard work
and a little help."

Cornelius worked hard
at learning the monkey's tricks,
and the monkey seemed happy
to help him.

When he had finally learned to stand on his head
and hang from his tail,
Cornelius walked proudly back to the riverbeach.

"Look!" he said. "I can stand on my head."
"So what!" was all the others said.

"And I can hang from my tail!"
said Cornelius.
But the others
just frowned and repeated,
"So what!"

Disappointed and angry,
Cornelius decided to go back to the monkey.
But just as he had turned around, he looked back.
And what did he see?

There the others were, falling all over themselves
trying to stand on their heads and hang from their tails!
Cornelius smiled. Life on the riverbeach
would never be the same again.

Leo Lionni was born in Holland and grew up in Italy. He received his Ph.D. in economics from the University of Genoa in 1935 and came to this country in 1939 with his wife, Nora, and their two young sons. He has been president of the American Institute of Graphic Arts, head of the graphic design department of the Parsons School of Design, co-editor of *Print* magazine, art director of *Fortune*, and, most recently, Critic-in-Residence at the Cooper Union School of Art.

He made his children's book debut in 1959 with the publication of *Little Blue and Little Yellow*. Since then he has written and illustrated forty picture books that have delighted children and won high critical acclaim the world over. Four of them— *Inch by Inch, Swimmy, Frederick*, and *Alexander and the Wind-Up Mouse*—have been chosen as Caldecott Honor Books.

The Lionnis divide their time between homes in Tuscany, Italy, and New York City.

TOLONO PUBLIC LIBRARY